THE COWS

Also by Lydia Davis

The Cows

Lydia Davis

Photographs

Lydia Davis
Theo Cote
Stephen Davis

QUARTERNOTE CHAPBOOK SERIES #9

Sarabande  Books
LOUISVILLE, KENTUCKY

Managing Editor
Sarabande Books, Inc.
2234 Dundee Road, Suite 200
Louisville, KY 40205

Library of Congress Cataloging-in-Publication Data

Davis, Lydia, 1947–
   The cows / by Lydia Davis. — 1st ed.
      p. cm. — (Quarternote chapbook series ; no. 9)
   ISBN 978-1-932511-93-2 (pbk. : alk. paper)
   1. Cows. I. Title.
   PS3554.A9356C69 2011
   813'.54—dc22

                                          2010025149

Manufactured in Canada.

10 9 8 7 6 5 4 3 2 1

This book is printed on acid-free paper.
Sarabande Books is a nonprofit literary organization.

This project is supported in part by an award from the National
Endowment for the Arts.

The Kentucky Arts Council, the state arts agency, supports
Sarabande Books with state tax dollars and federal funding
from the National Endowment for the Arts.

Photo Credits
Cover photo by Theo Cote; photos pp. 8, 10, 14, 17, 18, 21, 24, 28, 32-34, 37,
and title page by Lydia Davis; photos pp. 7, 16, 31, 36 by Theo Cote; photos
pp. 25, 26 by Stephen Davis

COVER AND TEXT DESIGN BY KIRKBY GANN TITTLE.

The Cows

EACH NEW DAY, when they come out from the far side of the barn, it is like the next act, or the start of an entirely new play.

They amble out from the far side of the barn with their rhythmic, graceful walk, and it is an occasion, like the start of a parade.

Sometimes the second and third come out in stately procession while the first has stopped and stands still, staring.

They come out from behind the barn as though something is going to happen, and then nothing happens.

Or we pull back the curtain in the morning and they are already there, in the early sunlight.

They are a deep, inky black. It is a black that swallows light.

Their bodies are entirely black, but they have white on their faces. On the faces of two of them, there are large patches of white, like a mask. On the face of the third, there is only a small patch on the forehead, the size of a silver dollar.

They are motionless until they move again, one foot and then another—fore, hind, fore, hind—and stop in another place, motionless again.

So often they are standing completely still. Yet when I look up again a few minutes later, they are in another place, again standing completely still.

When they all three stand bunched together in a far corner of the field by the woods, they form one dark irregular mass, with twelve legs.

They are often crowded together in the large field. But sometimes they lie down far apart from each other, evenly spaced over the grass.

Today, two appear halfway out from behind the barn, standing still. Ten minutes go by. Now they are all the way out, standing still. Another ten minutes go by. Now the third is out and they are all three in a line, standing still.

The third comes out into the field from behind the barn when the other two have already chosen their spots, quite far apart. She can choose to join either one. She goes deliberately to the one in the far corner. Does she prefer the company of that cow, or does she prefer that corner, or is it more complicated—that that corner seems more appealing because of the presence of that cow?

Their attention is complete, as they look across the road: They are still, and face us.

Just because they are so still, their attitude seems philosophical.

I see them most often out the kitchen window over the top of a hedge. My view of them is bounded on either side by leafy trees. I am surprised that the cows are so often visible, because the portion of the hedge over which I see them is only about three feet long, and, even more puzzling, if I hold my arm straight out in front of me, the field of my vision in which they are grazing is only the length of half a finger. Yet that field of vision contains a part of their grazing field that is hundreds of square feet in area.

That one's legs are moving, but because she is facing us directly she seems to be staying in one place. Yet she is getting bigger, so she must be coming this way.

One of them is in the foreground and two are farther back, in the middle ground between her and the woods. In my field of vision, they occupy together in the middle ground the same amount of space she occupies alone in the foreground.

Because there are three, one of them can watch what the other two are doing together.

Or, because there are three, two can worry about the third, for instance the one lying down. They worry about her even though she often lies down, even though they all often lie down. Now the two worried ones stand at angles to the other, with their noses down against her, until at last she gets up.

They are nearly the same size, and yet one is the largest, one the middle-sized, and one the smallest.

One thinks there is a reason to walk briskly to the far corner of the field, but the other thinks there is no reason, and stands still where she is.

At first she stands still where she is, while the other walks away briskly, but then she changes her mind, and follows.

She follows, but stops halfway there. Is it that she has forgotten why she was going there, or that she has lost interest? She and the other are standing in parallel positions. She is looking straight ahead.

How often they stand still and slowly look around as though they have never been here before

But now, in an access of emotion, she trots a few feet.

I see only one cow, by the fence. As I walk up to the fence, I see part of a second cow: one ear sticking sideways out the door of the barn. Soon, I know, her whole face will appear, looking at me.

They are not disappointed in us, or do not remember being disappointed. If, one day, when we have nothing to offer them, they lose interest and turn away, they will have forgotten their disappointment by the next day. We know, because they look up when we first appear, and don't look away.

Sometimes they advance as a group, in little relays.

One gains courage from the one in front of her and moves forward a few steps, passing her by just a little. Now the one farthest back gains courage from the one in front and moves forward until she, in turn, is the leader. And so in this way, taking courage from each other, they advance, as a group, toward the strange thing in front of them.

In this, functioning as a single entity, they are not unlike the small flock of pigeons we sometimes see over the railway station, wheeling and turning in the sky continuously, making immediate small group decisions about where to go next.

When we come close to them, they are curious and come forward. They want to look at us and smell us. Before they smell us, they blow out forcefully, to clear their passages.

They like to lick things — a person's hand or sleeve, or the head or shoulders or back of another cow. And they like to be licked: while she is being licked, she stands very still with her head slightly lowered and a look of deep concentration in her eyes.

One may be jealous of another being licked: she thrusts her head under the outstretched neck of the one licking, and butts upward till the licking stops.

Two of them are standing close together: now they both move at the same moment, shifting into a different position in relation to each other, and then stand still again, as if following exactly the instructions of a choreographer.

Now they shift so that there is a head at either end and two thick leg-clusters in between.

After staying with the others in a tight clump for some time, one walks away by herself to the far corner of the field: at this moment, she does seem to have a mind of her own.

Lying down, seen from the side, her head up, feet bent in front of her, she forms a long, very acute triangle.

Her head, from the side, is nearly an isosceles triangle, but with a blunted angle where her nose is.

In a moment of solitary levity, as she leads the way out across the field, she bucks once and then prances.

Two of them are beginning a lively game of butt-your-head when a car goes by and they stop to look.

She bucks, stiffly rocking back and forth. This excites another one to butt heads with her. After they are done butting heads, the other one puts her nose back down to the ground and this one stands still, looking straight ahead, as though wondering what she just did.

Forms of play: head butting; mounting, either at the back or at the front; trotting away by yourself; trotting together; going off bucking and prancing by yourself; resting your head and chest on the ground until they notice and trot toward you; circling each other; taking the position for head-butting and then not doing it.

She moos toward the wooded hills behind her, and the sound comes back. She moos again in a high falsetto. It is a very small sound to come from such a large, dark animal.

Today, they are positioned exactly one behind the next in a line, head to tail, head to tail, as though coupled like the cars of a railway train, the first looking straight forward like the headlight of the locomotive.

The shape of a black cow, seen directly head-on: a smooth black oval, larger at the top and tapering at the bottom to a very narrow extension, like a tear drop.

Standing with their back ends close together, now, they face three of the four cardinal points of the compass.

Sometimes one takes the position for defecating, her tail, raised, in the curved shape of a pump handle.

They seem expectant this morning, but it is a combination of two things: the strange yellow light before a storm and their alert expressions as they listen to a loud woodpecker.

Spaced out evenly over the pale yellow-green grass of late November, one, two, and three, they are so still, and their legs so thin, in comparison to their bodies, that when they stand sideways to us, sometimes their legs seem like prongs, and they seem stuck to the earth.

How flexible, and how precise, she is: she can reach one of her back hoofs all the way forward, to scratch a particular spot inside her ear.

It is the lowered head that makes her seem less noble than, say, a horse, or a deer surprised in the woods. More exactly, it is her lowered head and neck. As she stands still, the top of her head is level with her back, or even a little lower, and so she seems to be hanging her head in discouragement, embarrassment, or shame. There is at least a suggestion of humility and dullness about her. But all these suggestions are false.

He says to us: they don't really do anything.
Then he says: But of course there is not a lot for them to do.

Their grace: as they walk, they are more graceful when seen from the side than when seen from the front. Seen from the front, as they walk, they tip just a little from side to side.

When they are walking, their forelegs are more graceful than their back legs, which appear stiffer.

The forelegs are more graceful than the back legs because they lift in a curve, whereas the back legs lift in a jagged line like a bolt of lightning.

But perhaps the back legs, while less graceful than the forelegs, are more elegant.

It is because of the way the joints in the legs work: Whereas the two lower joints of the front leg bend the same way, so that the front leg as it is raised forms a curve, the two lower joints of the back leg bend in opposite directions, so that the leg, when raised, forms two opposite angles, the lower one gentle, pointing forward, the upper one sharp, pointing back.

Now, because it is winter, they are not grazing, but only standing still and staring, or, now and then, walking here and there.

It is a very cold winter morning, just above zero degrees, but sunny. Two of them stand still, head to tail, for a very long time, oriented roughly east-west. They are probably presenting their broad sides to the sun, for warmth.

If they finally move, is it because they are warm enough, or is it that they are stiff, or bored?

They are sometimes a mass of black, a lumpy black clump, against the snow, with a head at either end and many legs below.

Or the three of them, seen from the side, when they are all facing the same way, three deep, make one thick cow with three heads, two up and one lowered.

Sometimes, what we see against the snow is their bumps—bumps of ears and nose, bumps of bony hips, or the sharp bone on the top of their heads, or their shoulders.

If it snows, it snows on them the same way it snows on the trees and the field. Sometimes they are just as still as the trees or the field. The snow piles up on their backs and heads.

It has been snowing heavily for some time, and it is still snowing. When we go up to them, where they stand by the fence, we see that there is a layer of snow on their backs. There is also a layer of snow on their faces, and even a thin line of snow on each of the whiskers around their mouths. The snow on their faces is so white that now the white patches on their faces, which once looked so white against their black, are a shade of yellow.

Against the snow, in the distance, coming head-on this way, separately, spaced far apart, they are like wide black strokes of a pen.

A winter's day: First, a boy plays in the snow in the same field as the cows. Then, outside the field, three boys throw snowballs at a fourth boy who rides past them on a bike.

Meanwhile, the three cows are standing end to end, each touching the next, like paper cutouts.

Now the boys begin to throw snowballs at the cows. A neighbor watching says: "It was only a matter of time. They were bound to do it."

But the cows merely walk away from the boys.

They are so black on the white snow and standing so close together that I don't know if there are three there, together, or just two—but surely there are more than eight legs in that bunch?

At a distance, one bows down into the snow; the other two watch, then begin to trot toward her, then break into a canter.

At the far edge of the field, next to the woods, they are walking from right to left, and because of where they are, their dark bodies entirely disappear against the dark woods behind them, while their legs are still visible against the snow — black sticks twinkling against the white ground.

They are often like a math problem: 2 cows lying down in the snow, plus 1 cow standing up looking at the hill, equals 3 cows.

Or 1 cow lying down in the snow, plus 2 cows on their feet looking this way across the road, equals 3 cows.

Today, they are all three lying down.

Now, in the heart of winter, they spend a lot of time lying around in the snow.

Does she lie down because the other two have lain down before her, or are they all three lying down because they all feel it is the right time to lie down? (It is just after noon, on a chilly, early spring day, with intermittent sun and no snow on the ground.)

Is the shape of her lying down, when seen from the side, most of all like a boot-jack as seen from above?

It is hard to believe a life could be so simple, but it is just this simple. It is the life of a ruminant, a protected domestic ruminant. If she were to give birth to a calf, though, her life would be more complicated.

The cows in the past, the present, and the future: They were so black against the pale yellow-green grass of late November. Then they were so black against the white snow of winter. Now they are so black against the tawny grass of early spring. Soon, they will be so black against the dark green grass of summer.

Two of them are probably pregnant, and have probably been pregnant for many months. But it is hard to be sure, because they are so massive. We won't know until the calf is born. And after the calf is born, even though it will be quite large, the cow will seem to be just as massive as she was before.

The angles of a cow as she grazes, seen from the side: from her bony hips to her shoulders, there is a very gradual, barely perceptible slope down, then, from her shoulders to the tip of her nose, down in the grass, a very steep slope.

The position, or form, itself, of the grazing cow, when seen from the side, is graceful.

Why do they so often graze side-view on to me, rather than front- or rear-view on? Is it so that they can keep an eye on both the woods, on one side, and the road, on the other? Or does the traffic on the road, sparse though it is, right to left, and left to right, influence them so that they graze parallel to it?

Or perhaps it isn't true that they graze more often sideways on to me. Maybe I simply pay more attention to them when they are sideways on. After all, when they are perfectly sideways on, to me, the greatest surface area of their bodies is visible to me; as soon as the angle changes, I see less of them, until, when they are perfectly end-on or front-on to me, the least of them is visible.

They make slow progress here and there in the field, with only their tails moving briskly from side to side. In contrast, little flocks of birds—as black as they are—fly up and land constantly in waves behind and around them. The birds move with what looks to us like joy or exhilaration but is probably simply keenness in pursuit of their prey-- the flies that in turn dart out from the cows and settle on them again.

Their tails do not exactly whip or flap, and they do not swish, since there is no swishing sound. There is a swooping or looping motion to them, with a little fillip at the end, from the tasseled part.

There used to be three dark horizontal lumps on the field when they lay down to rest. Now there are three and another very small one.

Soon he, three days old, is grazing, too, or learning to graze, but so small, from where I stand watching him, that he is sometimes hidden by a twig.

When he stands still, a miniature, nose to the grass like his mother, because his body is still so small and his legs so thin, he looks like a thick black staple.

When he runs after her, he canters like a rocking horse.

They do sometimes protest—when they have no water, or can't get into the barn. One of them, usually the darkest, will moo in a perfectly regular blast twenty or more times in succession. The sound echoes off the hills like a fire alarm coming from a fire house.

At these times, she sounds authoritative. But she has no authority.

A second calf is born, to a second cow. Now, one small dark lump in the grass is the older calf. Another, smaller dark lump in the grass is the newborn calf.

The third cow could not be bred because she would not get into the van to be taken to the bull. Then, after a few months, they wanted to take her to be slaughtered. But she would not get into the van to be taken to slaughter. So she is still there.

Other neighbors may be away, from time to time, but the cows are always there, in the field. Or, if they are not in the field, they are in the barn.

I know that if they are in the field, and if I go up to the fence on this side, they will, all three, sooner or later come up to the fence on the other side, to meet me.

They do not know the words "person," "neighbor," "watch," or even "cow."

At dusk, when our light is on indoors, they can't be seen, though they are there in the field across the road. If we turn off the light, and look out into the dusk, gradually they can be seen again.

They are still out there, grazing, at dusk. But as the dusk turns to dark, while the sky above the woods is still a purplish blue, it is harder and harder to see their black bodies against the darkening field. Then they can't be seen at all, but they are still out there, grazing in the dark.

Theo Cote

Lydia Davis, a 2003 MacArthur Fellow, is the author, most recently, of *The Collected Stories* (Farrar, Straus & Giroux, 2009). She is also the latest translator of *Swann's Way* by Marcel Proust (Viking Penguin, 2002), and *Madame Bovary* by Gustave Flaubert (Viking Penguin, 2010). She lives in rural upstate New York and teaches at SUNY Albany, where she is also a Fellow of the New York State Writers Institute.